Daisy Lewis has written an entertaining book for children that also carries a powerful life-changing message to give kids power over their own lives and the thoughts that create those lives. Bring this book to every child you care about.

—Steve Chandler, author *The Story of You*

Published by Tate Publishing & Enterprises, LLC
127 E. Trade Center Terrace | Mustang, Oklahoma 73064 USA
1.888.361.9473 | www.tatepublishing.com

Tate Publishing is committed to excellence in the publishing industry. The company reflects the philosophy established by the founders, based on Psalm 68:11,
"The Lord gave the word and great was the company of those who published it."

Published in the United States of America

ISBN: 978-1-61739-540-6
1. Juvenile Fiction / Animals / Dogs
2. Ages 0-4
10.11.30

Pequeno Don Cisco

Daisy Lewis

Tate Publishing
& Enterprises

Once upon a time there was a tiny pup.
He was all alone. He wanted to give up.

He wanted people to see how he felt inside.
No one ever did, no matter how hard he tried.

He lived in a cage and his face was so sad.
This tiny pup was just a fad.

Month after month, so lonely and blue
He felt trapped, not knowing what to do.

Then, one day, in the midst of despair
He had a dream that filled the air.

With colors and rainbows and explosions of light!
He saw his future with all his *might!*

His name made him proud. He would say it out loud:
"I am Pequeño Don Cisco, the little dog hero."

And over and over his name he would say
He knew he was special; he'd be happy some day.

He never let up, not one single time,
And over and over he chanted this rhyme.

"My name is Pequeño Don Cisco.
"My mission is to be the little dog hero.

"I am not like any other dogs before.
"I have a special purpose to be so much more.

"I dream to find that special lady who will know who I am.
"I will never give up. I am Pequeño Don Cisco; yes, I am!"

His dreams became brighter; his visions he could see
He felt the happiness of how it would be.

There was a loud knock at the door; he felt his heart leap.
It woke him up from a very sound sleep.

He was taken upstairs, and to his surprise
He saw a face with the most beautiful eyes.

She had long, flowing hair and a shy little face.
The feeling he felt, he will never erase.

He looked into her eyes, and as strange as it seems,
He had to let her know. *"You have been in my dreams."*

And in an instant with a flash and a blinding light
The universe gave him all his might.

His thoughts and his visions had all come true.
His thoughts became things. That's his mission for you.

Happiness has become the fuel for his life.
Pretty Chiquita is now his wife.

They laugh, they play, they giggle, and they pray.
Their life is his dream in every way.

And then one day, by complete surprise,
Three puppies were born with the most beautiful eyes.

They looked like Chiquita. It happened so fast.
Pequeno Don Cisco had his family at last!

He felt so proud; he felt so glad.
He shouted over and over, "I am finally a dad!"

Their energy triumphant, one could not miss.
They had achieved a life of total bliss.

Pequeño Don Cisco and Chiquita, soul mates from the start,
Had created a mission with their heart.

The moral of this story began with a tiny pup
So miserable and blue, who wanted to give up.

But he changed his thoughts, and his dreams came true
His mission is to show how this can happen for you.

He was blessed with a gift that happiness brings
To teach our children that their thoughts become things.

e|LIVE

listen|imagine|view|experience

AUDIO BOOK DOWNLOAD INCLUDED WITH THIS BOOK!

In your hands you hold a complete digital entertainment package. In addition to the paper version, you receive a free download of the audio version of this book. Simply use the code listed below when visiting our website. Once downloaded to your computer, you can listen to the book through your computer's speakers, burn it to an audio CD or save the file to your portable music device (such as Apple's popular iPod) and listen on the go!

How to get your free audio book digital download:

1. Visit www.tatepublishing.com and click on the e|LIVE logo on the home page.
2. Enter the following coupon code:
   5c7e-8a0e-6ef3-87fe-929a-77a2-4080-319d
3. Download the audio book from your e|LIVE digital locker and begin enjoying your new digital entertainment package today!